To Bailey,
Be true to your
story!

Karen A Mo[...]

MW00953259

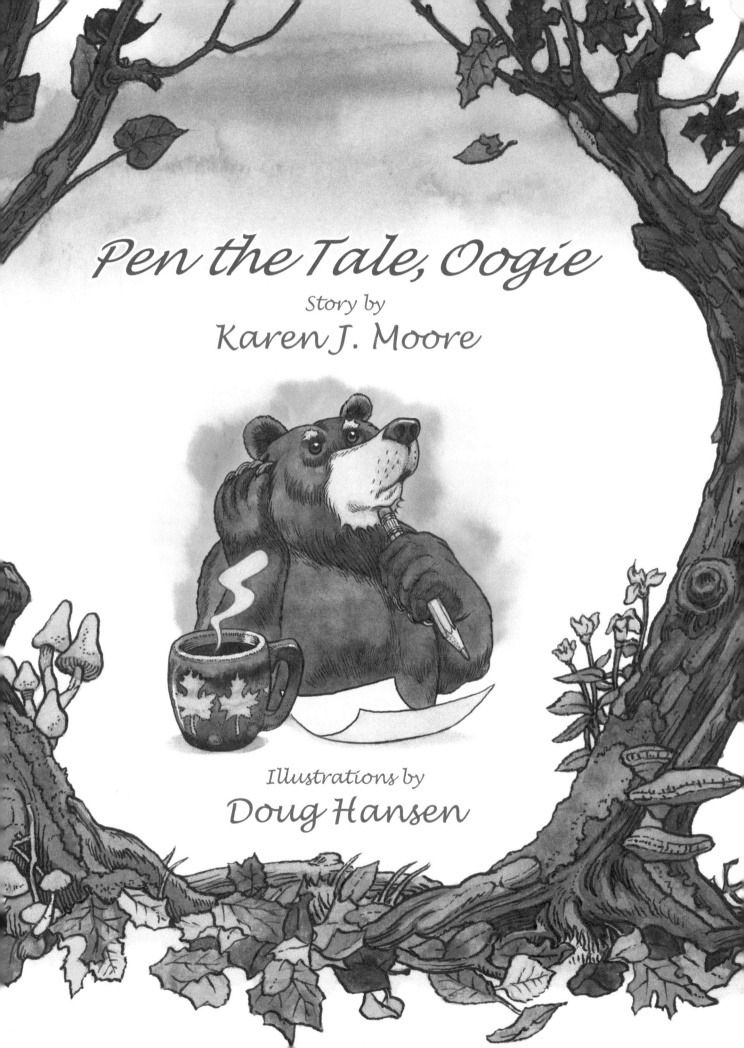

Pen the Tale, Oogie

Story by
Karen J. Moore

Illustrations by
Doug Hansen

Pen the Tale, Oogie

Hardcover ISBN: 978-1-943050-35-2
Paperback ISBN: 978-1-943050-34-5

December 2016

Barn Owl Media is a wholly owned imprint of HBE Publishing

All inquiries should be addressed to:

HBE Publishing
640 Clovis Ave
Clovis, CA, 93612

http://www.hbepublishing.com

HBE PUBLISHING

Printed in U.S.A

Dedication:

Every good gift and every perfect gift is from above . . .

James 1:17 KJV

To my little huggie bears: Addison, Ashlyn, Gavin, and Brynlee—Nonny loves you forever and always.

KJM

Dedicated to every artist and writer with a story to tell.

DH

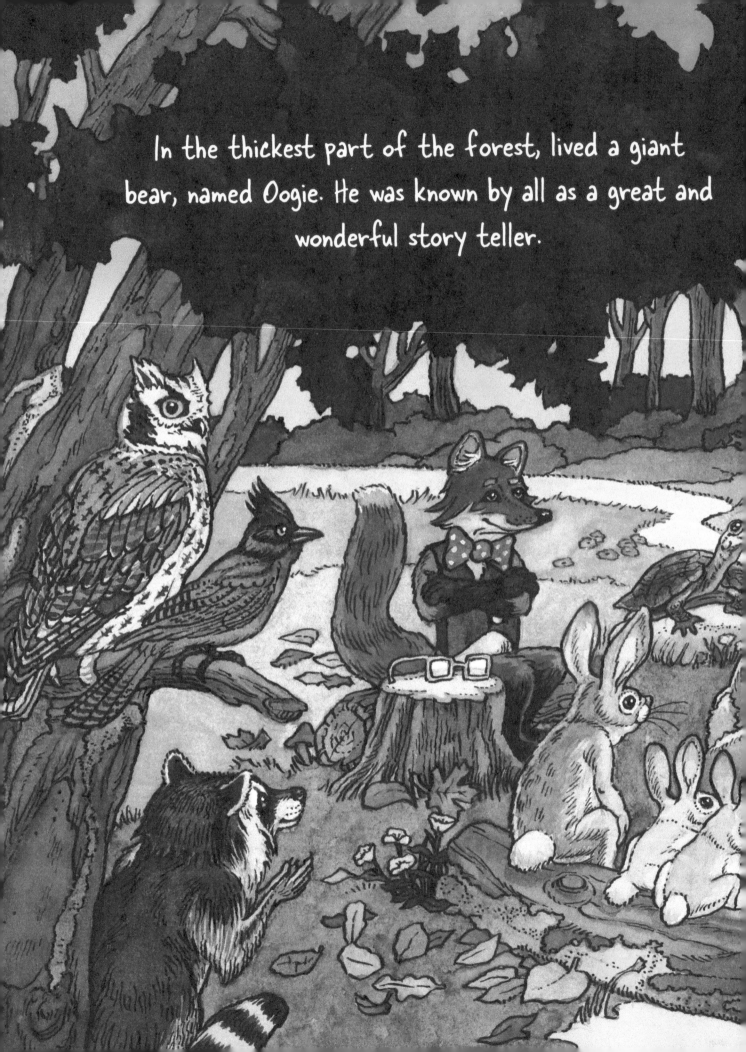

In the thickest part of the forest, lived a giant bear, named Oogie. He was known by all as a great and wonderful story teller.

One night, as Oogie told his tales, he tasted the first chill of winter. He knew time was running short.

When everyone left, he began to pace and fret. "What's wrong, Oogie?" asked Mr. Fox, who had come back to look for his glasses.

"The time for my winter nap is fast approaching. What will the animals do without their nightly tales?"

Mr. Fox loved solving problems,
so he joined Oogie in pacing and
fretting, fretting and pacing.

"I have an idea," said Mr. Fox. "Why don't you write your stories down? Then, everyone can read them while you hibernate."

"I've never written my stories before," said Oogie.
"Do you think I can?"

"Of course," said Mr. Fox. "You do the writing
and I'll take care of everything else."

They made a plan, and Oogie went home to write.

As he sat drinking his hot chocolate, he stared at the paper.
He tapped his pencil. He twiddled his thumbs.
He stared at the ceiling.

NOTHING.

He went for a walk, and the crisp night air led to an idea.
A charming story about a family of bears who came home
from a walk and found an intruder in their den.

Pleased, he placed it outside for Mr. Fox.

The next morning, Mr. Fox pushed his way through the door.
"No, no, no! Haven't you read,
Goldilocks and the Three Bears?"

"No, I don't believe I have."
"Well it's been done . . . a lot," said Mr. Fox.

"Grrrrr," Oogie growled at the word: REJECTED.

That night he sharpened his pencils, straightened his papers, and cleared his desk.

Again . . . NOTHING.

He made something to eat, and the thick honey sandwich gave him a thought.

He wrote about a cuddly little bear, with lots of friends, who always found trouble while searching for honey.

In the morning, Mr. Fox thumped the burrs from his tail and asked, "Don't you remember THAT famous bear and his honey pot?"

"No, I can't say that I do."

"It's been told,"
said Mr. Fox shaking his head.

"Grrrrrr," Oogie did not like the word: REJECTED.

Oogie prepared his bed, swept the floor, and looked for his napping hat.

"That's it!" he said,
and sat to write a funny story about a
traveling bear who wears a yellow hat.

"You are," said Mr. Fox adjusting his glasses.
"Remember Oogie, the best stories come from your heart."

Oogie gazed at the moon
        and listened to the night sounds.

He closed his eyes and
drifted off, just a little,
and found the place
where stories are born.

The stories kept coming,
one after the other.

He wrote about a chipmunk who saves the day.

He wrote about a raccoon who catches a thief.

He even wrote scary stories to keep the night animals awake.
He wrote . . . and wrote . . . and wrote.

The next morning, Mr. Fox jumped up and down.
"Yes, yes, yes!" his tail quivered with excitement.
"These new stories have something for everyone."

Oogie danced when he saw the word: ACCEPTED.

Then, he yawned and said,
"Thank you, Mr. Fox."

As he settled in for his long winter nap, Oogie drifted back to that magical place of imagination, where great and wonderful stories blossom like spring flowers.

Acknowledgments

My thanks and gratitude to:

God, for all my blessings.

My forever sweetheart and husband, Rick, for loving and cheering me on.

Dan and Peggy Dunklee, for taking a chance on me. You'll never know what it has meant to me.

Doug Hanson, for breathing beautiful life into our characters, you are a master.

Chris Estep, for your technical expertise.

Janice Stevens, for your gentle guidance and mentorship.

My Writing for Publication classmates, I've learned so much from each of you.

Sassy Scribes, my kidlit soulmates.

The staff at A Book Barn, you guys rock.

My Mom, Dad, and brother, for believing in me—always.

My children, Justin and Rashelle, their spouses, Charlotte and Mike, and my grandchildren, for all the love, surprises, and adventure you've brought to my life.

Anne, Kathy, and Gayle, my writing and travelling buddies and partners in crime.

Linda Norris, my webmaster and dear friend.

SCBWI, especially my regional advisor, Bitsy Kemper, for critiquing an earlier draft of Oogie.

Deb and Rob, for always listening and offering help.

My many close and wonderful friends, for encouraging and supporting me over the years.

I love you all.

KJM

Acknowledgments

Dan and Peggy Dunklee are ardent champions of literature and literacy. They are ambitious publishers with high hopes, thriving hometown book merchants, and generous patrons of the regional literary scene. Readers, authors, and book-lovers benefit from A Book Barn calendar that bristles with book-related activities. Aficionados of every literary genre are welcome under their roof and are ably looked after by the friendly and involved staff.

I appreciate that the Dunklees understand the role pictures can play in storytelling. I gratefully acknowledge that, as editor, Dan allowed me the time and creative flexibility I needed to illustrate a suitable world for Oogie and Mr. Fox.

Karen Moore wrote the charming story that describes Oogie's creative struggles. We have all tried, like Oogie, to create something that is personal, original, and connects with our fellows. We all want Oogie to succeed; if he can triumph, so can we. Karen's hopeful fable of the creative process suited me and I was pleased that my illustrations would become part of the story of Oogie the bear.

Doug Hansen

About the Author

Karen J. Moore

Karen is a wife, mother, and grandmother of four. She worked for many years as a literacy tutor and Title I Instructional Aide. She loves to read, go to the movies, and spend time with friends and family. She lives in the Central California foothills with her husband and Australian Shepherd, Shay.

About the Illustrator

Doug Hansen

Illustrator Doug Hansen was born in Fresno, California and is the eldest of six children in an artistic family. He was a newsroom artist at The Fresno Bee newspaper for 23 years. The Bee published two collections of his Fresno Sketchbook pen and ink drawings of Valley landmarks.

Hansen received both his BA and MA in Art from California State University, Fresno. He is a professor of illustration in the Graphic Design area in the Department of Art and Design at Fresno State.

Hansen illustrated two books of essays by Del Rey author David "Mas" Masumoto: Letters to the Valley: A Harvest of Memories, and Heirlooms: Letters from a Peach Farmer.

Doug's own "California-centric" children's books include: Mother Goose in California, Aesop in California, and California, the Magic Island.

Hansen lives and works in Clovis, CA, and particularly enjoys using the watercolor and ink techniques employed in Pen the Tale, Oogie.

Photo Credit: Nat Hansen

Teacher's Resources

Pen the Tale, Oogie: A Classroom Guide and Support for Teachers
Vocabulary—Giving Words Meaning and Giving Meaning to Words
Flesch-Kincaid Grade Level 3.5

This strategy was created to help teachers familiarize students with the vocabulary words in a given book or unit being taught. Each step is a guide to help students make sense of the words they come across in their reading.

Step 1—Introduction
   a) write the word on the whiteboard
   b) read the word to the class
   c) ask students to repeat
   d) example "The word is fret. What's the word?" Class responds, "The word is fret."

Step 2—Student friendly definition
   a) teacher states the word, then gives the class word definition
   b) example: "fret: means to worry about something"
   c) students repeat the definition of the word
   d) when possible the teacher should also show a picture of the word (good for second language students and visual learners)

Step 3—Rephrase the definition,
   a) teacher reads a sentence and students supply the new word.
   b) example "The baseball player began to _____ about the next ball being pitched."

Step 4—Provide other examples
   a) teacher reads the second sentence
   b) teacher demonstrates using Total Physical Response TPR
   c) teacher illustrates word

Step 5—Check for understanding
   a) partner time—share the definition with your shoulder partner
   b) tell a time when you . . .
   c) quiz your neighbor on the new words

Pen the Tale, Oogie
Vocabulary Guide

What's another word for?

1. **fret**—fuss, worry, agonize

2. **approaching**—creeping up, beginning, advancing

3. **hibernate**—sleep, hide away, vegetate

4. **twiddled**—fiddled, messed with, toyed with

5. **intruder**—prowler, trespasser snooper

6. **rejected**—refused, declined, dismissed

7. **burrs**—stickers, prickly weed

8. **magical**—enchanted, mystical, wonderful

9. **quivered**—shook, wiggled, trembled

10. **blossomed**—developed, came to life, grew

11. **accepted**—approved, agreed upon, wanted

Pen the Tale, Oogie: Teacher's Notes

Part One—Getting Ready

A) Pre Reading Activities (Based on students' interests and abilities.)
1. Show the cover to the class and read them the title of the book.
2. Prepare them for the story by talking about:
   - Animals that live in a forest—brainstorm for later use
   - What a tale is and where it comes from-brainstorm favorite tales
3. Journal writing prompt. *"My favorite forest animal"* or *"Once upon a time, . . ."*

B) Introducing new vocabulary words
Teacher instructions: Listen to the word, listen to the sentence, then let's try to figure out what the word means together.
   - fret: *"When everyone left, he began to pace and <u>fret</u>."*
   - approaching: *"The time for my long winter nap is fast <u>approaching</u>."*
   - hibernate: *"Then, everyone can read them while you <u>hibernate</u>."*
   - twiddled: *"He tapped his pencil, <u>twiddled</u> his thumbs and stared at the ceiling."*
   - intruder: *"They came home from a walk and found they had an <u>intruder</u>."*
   - rejected: *"Oogie growled at the word: <u>rejected</u>."*
   - burrs: *"Mr. Fox thumped the <u>burrs</u> from his tail."*
   - magical: *"Then, he closed his eyes and found the <u>magical</u> place where stories are born."*
   - accepted: *"Oogie danced when he saw the word: <u>accepted</u>."*
   - blossomed: *"wonderful stories <u>blossomed</u> like the coming spring."*

Part Two—During Reading

1. For kindergarten and possibly first grade, use this story as a read aloud asking questions to check for understanding during the reading.
2. For some first grade and most of second grade this story can but used either as a read aloud, small group, or whole group literature activity.
3. Comprehension Questions to ask during reading (CFU) or once story has been read.
4. What is Oogie's talent? Do you have a special talent?
   - Do you think the title, Pen the Tale, Oogie, helps you figure out what the story will be about? Explain your answer.
   - What does Mr. Fox suggest Oogie try to do?
   - Who do you think will read Oogie's stories while he is in hibernation?

Part Three—Closure (Ideas to help students better understand story structure, sequence of events and character analysis.)

1. Elements of story: identify the main characters
2. Discuss real vs. make believe
3. Identify the setting for the story.
4. Identify the problem and the solution.
5. Bring in personal elements by prompting students to talk about or write about a time when they felt the need to help others like Oogie did in this story.
6. Research class or individual project: from list of forest animals created before reading story, ask students to pick one and find out facts. Create a flip book with one detail on each page.
7. Compare and contrast: fold paper in half label ½ country the other ½ forest and draw a picture of a country (farm) scene and a picture of a forest.

Pen the Tale, Oogie: A Classroom Guide and Support for Teachers
Common Core State Standards
Flesch-Kincaid Grade Level 3.5

Kindergarten—Use as a read aloud with your class.
Strand: Reading Literature

Key Ideas and Details
- K.RL.1
- K.RL.3

Craft and Structure
- K.RL.4 (approaching, fret, hibernate, twiddled, intruder, rejected, burrs, magical, images, quivered, accepted, blossomed)
- K.RL.6

Integration of Knowledge and Ideas
- K.RL.7

Strand: Reading Informational

Key Ideas and Details
- K.RI.1
- K.RI.2
- K.RI.3

Craft and Structure
- K.RI.4 (approaching, fret, hibernate, twiddled, intruder, rejected, burrs, magical, quivered, accepted, blossomed)
- K.RI.5
- K.RI.6

Integration of Knowledge and Ideas
- K.RI.7
- K.RI.8

Strand: Reading Foundational

Print Concepts
- K.RF.1

Phonics and word Recognition
- K.RF.3.c

Strand: Writing

Text Types and Purposes
- K.W.1
- K.W.3

Strand: Speaking and Listening

Comprehension and Collaboration
- K.SL.1
- K.SL.3

Strand: Language

Vocabulary Acquisition and Use
- K.L.4.a and b
- K.L.5.c and d

Pen the Tale, Oogie: A Classroom Guide and Support for Teachers
Common Core State Standards
Flesch-Kincaid Grade Level 3.5

First Grade—Use as a read aloud with your class, or a challenge for high readers
Strand: Reading Literature

Key Ideas and Details
- 1.RL.1
- 1.RL.2
- 1.RL.3

Craft and Structure
- 1.RL.4
- 1.RL.6

Integration of Knowledge and Ideas
- 1.RL.7
- 1.RL.9

Strand: Reading Informational

Key Ideas and Details
- 1.RI.1
- 1.RI.2
- 1.RI.3

Craft and Structure
- 1.RI.4 (approaching, fret, hibernate, twiddled, intruder, rejected, burrs, magical, quivered, accepted, blossomed)
- 1.RI.6

Integration of Knowledge and Ideas
- 1.RI.7
- 1.RI.8

Strand: Reading Foundational

Print Concepts
- 1.RF.1

Fluency
- 1.RF.4

Strand: Writing

Text Types and Purposes
- 1.W.1
- 1.W.3

Strand: Speaking and Listening

Comprehension and Collaboration
- 1.SL.1
- 1.SL.2

Presentation of Knowledge and Ideas
- 1.SL.4
- 1.SL.5
- 1.SL.6

Strand: Language

Conventions of Standard English
- 1.L.1

Vocabulary Acquisition and Use
- 1.L.4.a (approaching, fret, hibernate, twiddled, intruder, rejected, burrs, magical, quivered, accepted, blossomed)
- 1.L.6

Pen the Tale, Oogie: A Classroom Guide and Support for Teachers
Common Core State Standards
Flesch-Kincaid Grade Level 3.5

Second Grade – Use as a read aloud with your class, or a challenge for high readers

Strand: Reading Literature

Key Ideas and Details
- 2.RL.1
- 2.RL.3

Craft and Structure
- 2.RL.5
- 2.RL.6

Integration of Knowledge and Ideas
- 2.RL.7

Strand: Reading Informational

Key Ideas and Details
- 2.RI.1
- 2.RI.3

Craft and Structure
- 2.RI.4 (approaching, fret, hibernate, twiddled, intruder, rejected, burrs, magical, quivered, accepted, blossomed)
- 2.RI.5
- 2.RL.6

Integration of Knowledge and Ideas
- 2.RI.7
- 2.RI.8

Strand: Reading Foundational

Fluency
- 2.RF.4

Strand: Writing

Text Types and Purposes
- 2.W.1
- 2.W.3

Strand: Speaking and Listening

Comprehension and Collaboration
- 2.SL.1
- 2.SL.2

Presentation of Knowledge and Ideas
- 2.SL.5
- 2.SL.6

Strand: Language

Conventions of Standard English
- 2.L.1

Knowledge of Language
- 2.L.3

Vocabulary Acquisition and Use
- 2.L.4.a (approaching, fret, hibernate, twiddled, intruder, rejected, burrs, magical, quivered, accepted, blossomed)
- 2.L.5
- 2.L.6

CPSIA information can be obtained
at www.ICGtesting.com
Printed in the USA
BVHW020450260522
637894BV00002B/49

9 781943 050345